P is for Pirate

A Pirate Alphabet

Written by Eve Bunting and Illustrated by John Manders

For Keelin, aged five, our pirate girl.

—Eve

✕

For Trinity, Eulalia, and Andrew

—John

Text Copyright © 2014 Eve Bunting
Illustration Copyright © 2014 John Manders

Sleeping Bear Press™
315 E. Eisenhower Parkway, Suite 200
Ann Arbor, MI 48108
www.sleepingbearpress.com

Printed and bound in the United States.

10 9 8 7 6 5 4 3 2 1

Library of Congress Cataloging-in-Publication Data

Bunting, Eve, 1928-
P is for pirate : a pirate alphabet / written by Eve Bunting ;
illustrated by John Manders.
pages cm
ISBN 978-1-58536-815-0
1. Pirates—History—Juvenile literature. 2. Piracy--History—Juvenile literature.
3. Alphabet—Juvenile literature. I. Manders, John, ill. II. Title.
G535.B85 2014
910.4'5—dc23
2013050683

Introduction

There have always been pirates, as long as there have been men filled with greed and the lust for treasure.

As early as AD 400, Chinese and Japanese pirates prowled the seas around China and Southeast Asia. Their ships were junks, flat-bottomed, three-masted boats with sails of woven bamboo. By the Middle Ages piracy was well established as a "profession" in the Pacific and Atlantic oceans.

By the end of the seventeenth century pirates roved the seas of the world. They preyed on ships carrying gold and silver from South America. They plundered galleons from Africa filled with ivory and looted ships from the East Indies laden with silks and jewels and spices. This was indeed the "Golden Age of Piracy." So much so that by the middle of the sixteenth century most fishermen in England had a second source of income, piracy, which they called the "sweet trade"!

No one who sailed on the seas at any time was safe from marauders. The young Julius Caesar who ruled Rome from 49 to 44 BC was captured by pirates in the Mediterranean Sea in 75 BC.

The Golden Age of Piracy is long gone. But the stories and the legends, the tales of the pirates and their ships live on.

"The schooners and the merry crews
are laid away to rest
A little south the sunset
in the islands of the Blest."*

*From "A Ballad of John Silver" by John Masefield.

A is for the Articles (the code of conduct)

The rules were there
to see and sign.
Obey them,
and you might be fine.

A a

It is hard to believe that a bunch of pirates would have a code of conduct, rules to live by on a pirate ship. But they did. The "rules" were sworn to by each crew member and had to be obeyed.

Each ship had its own rules, but they were similar. They included such laws as that every man should have an equal vote on all important matters. That no man should gamble at dice or cards, that all candles be put out at eight at night, and that no pirate should strike another on board the ship. The captain and the quartermaster would be given the biggest share of the prizes taken and the rest divided according to rank. The ship musicians were allowed to rest on Sundays but should be available every other day. Yes, there were musicians on pirate ships!

These sound like rules for a scout camp. But a pirate ship was no scout camp. Sitting on cannons, the men swore on bibles, on skulls, or on crossed pistols to keep the code. Their signed names or their marks made it official.

Punishments for breaking the code were ruthless. Flogging, leg irons, keelhauling, or worse (See F.). The most severe could get you marooned on a desert island to die of hunger and thirst while your ship sailed away forever across the far horizon.

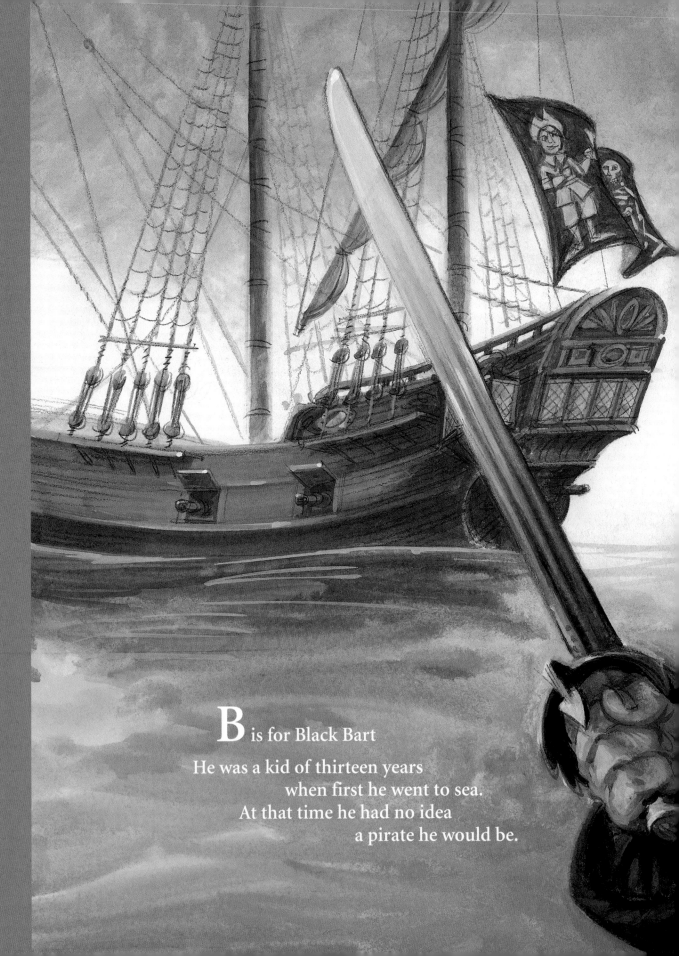

John Roberts was his real name. For some reason he changed the first name to Bartholomew. Perhaps he thought that was more distinguished. It was not until after his death that he was commonly referred to as Black Bart.

When the ship on which he was third mate was captured by pirates, Roberts was forced to join the pirate crew. "In an honest service there is thin commons, low wages and hard labor," he said once and finished by announcing, "No, a merry life and a short one shall be my motto."

As an excellent navigator he was very valuable. When the captain of the *Royal Rover* was shot, Roberts was voted into the job. History judges him to be the most successful pirate of the Golden Age.

Bb

B is for Black Bart

He was a kid of thirteen years
when first he went to sea.
At that time he had no idea
a pirate he would be.

Roberts was a ruthless captain and was not squeamish about torturing captives to get what he wanted. By 1721 he had a squadron of four ships under his command and was in control of hundreds of men.

His crew believed he was "pistol proof" because he came through so many battles uninjured. But he was not. When his ship was attacked by the *Swallow* he was struck in the throat by grapeshot and died on the deck. The crew member who found him, collapsed across the blocks and tackles of a gun, burst into tears. He was buried at sea. It is believed that Roberts's death marked the end of the Golden Age of Piracy.

A cutlass was the pirate's weapon of choice. It was a short, broad slashing sword, good to use when boarding an enemy vessel. It was strong enough to hack off ropes or canvas sails and sharp enough to kill a member of the other crew. Pirates and cutlasses seem to go naturally together.

There were also pistols. When a pirate went into battle he didn't just carry one, he carried several. Flintlock pistols didn't always fire the way they were supposed to. It was wise to have a backup. Not only that, but a shouting, cutlass-wielding pirate, heavily armed with cutlass, knife, and several pistols, was often enough to scare an enemy even before the fighting started! Pistols were often carried stuck into a sash slung around the shoulders. That left the hands free for other weapons that could be easily reached when needed.

Another deadly weapon was the grenade shell. Sometimes called "pomegranates" or "pirate flasks" the grenades were hollow, filled with gunpowder, and tossed into an enemy ship. They could be made of wood or iron. Boom! Smash!

The phrase "armed to the teeth" may have been coined to describe a pirate, armed with cutlass and pistols, boarding a vessel with a knife clasped between his teeth.

C
c

C is for Cutlass (and other weapons)

A cutlass, pistol, grappling hook,
a sharp and wicked knife.
These are all a pirate needs
to lead a pirate life.

D d

D is for Davy Jones's Locker

If you drowned you'd surely go
to that dreaded place below.
Davy Jones was waiting there
in his underwater lair.

"Davy Jones's Locker" is sailor slang for the bottom of the ocean. No one knows for certain who Davy Jones was, or why his name became associated with a drowning death. For example,

"*Where's ol' Billy Bosun?*"

"*Have you not heard? He's down in Davy Jones's Locker!*"

In 1751 author Tobias Smollett wrote, "According to the mythology of sailors, [Davy Jones] is the fiend who presides over all the evil spirits of the deep." According to Smollett he perches along the rigging on the eves of hurricanes, shipwrecks, etc., giving warning of what's to come.

Aargh! Pirates especially feared going down to Davy Jones's Locker since few of them could swim.

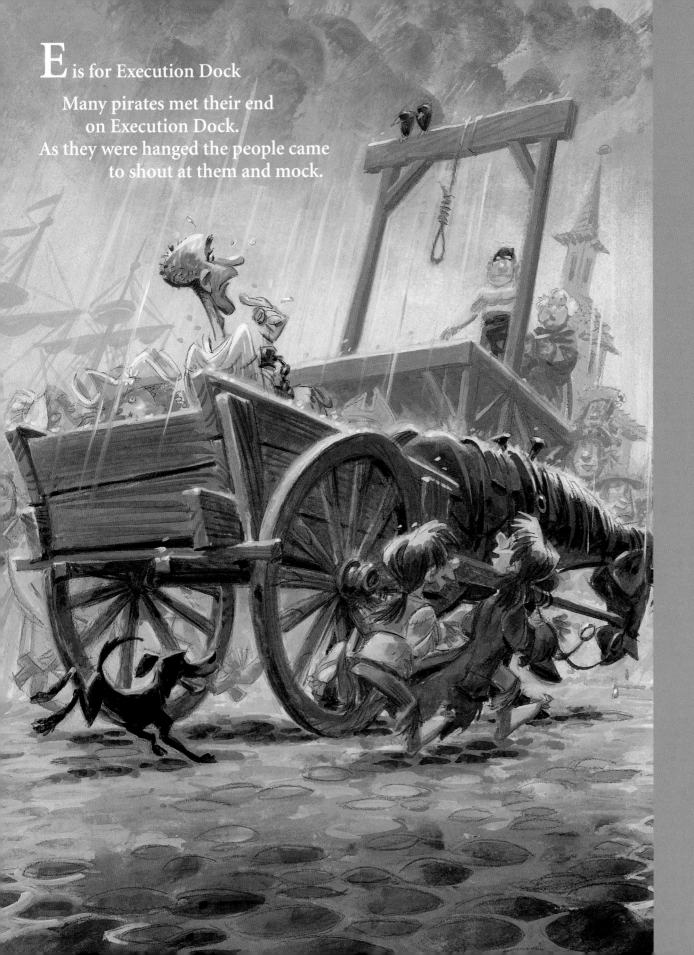

E is for Execution Dock

Many pirates met their end
on Execution Dock.
As they were hanged the people came
to shout at them and mock.

E e

Execution Dock was, and still is, a spot near Wapping on the river Thames, a mile from the Tower of London. It's no longer a place of execution. Now a British pub overlooks the spot where many pirates were once hanged.

When a hanging was scheduled, a crowd would gather on the shore. Boats were moored out on the river to be sure of a good view.

The pirate was brought in a cart to be hanged. A preacher came, too.

The pirate was allowed to address the crowds. Some repented, some were defiant to the end. The condemned man was permitted to hold a small bunch of flowers brought by a friend.

"Dancing the hempen jig," the pirates called it with fake bravado. None of them hoped to be asked to dance.

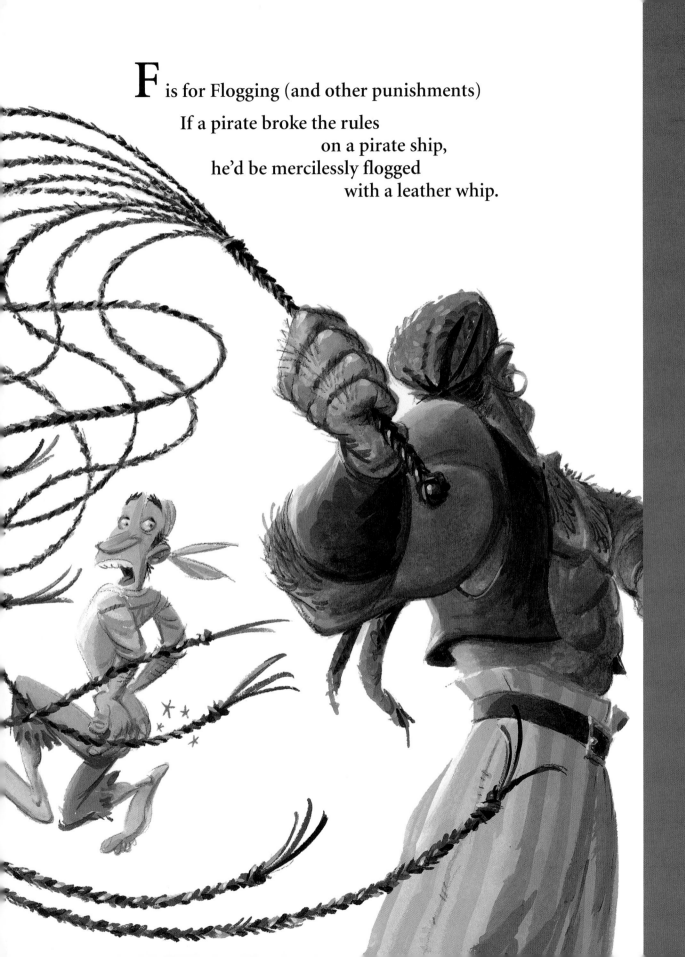

F is for Flogging (and other punishments)

If a pirate broke the rules
on a pirate ship,
he'd be mercilessly flogged
with a leather whip.

Punishments for pirates *by* pirates were extremely harsh. According to their code of conduct, a crew member who broke the code could be put in irons, flogged, keelhauled, or marooned.

Floggings were given by the quartermaster often using the cat o'nine tails, a whip with nine long leather thongs on the end. Sometimes the thongs were knotted. When it wasn't in use, "the cat" was kept in a bag, which is one explanation for the saying, "Don't let the cat out of the bag."

Keelhauling was worse. The guilty pirate was stripped of his clothes, had two ropes tied to his body, and was thrown overboard. A crewman on one side of the ship and one on the other pulled him back and forth under the ship's keel where barnacles were embedded. The barnacles tore his skin into shreds. Sometimes he drowned.

To be marooned was the worst punishment of all. The pirate, or "maroon" as they called him, would be put ashore on a desert island to die of hunger and thirst, extreme heat or cold.

Kindness was rare in pirate hearts.

F f

G g

G is for Gold! (and silver, too)

We like silver;
Gold is best.
We like treasure
in a chest.

Gold and silver. The very words made pirates lick their lips. Doubloons, each containing seven grams of gold, were most desired, and then silver pieces of eight. (One piece was worth eight *reales*, Spanish coins of lesser value.)

When loot was taken from another ship it was divided according to the code of conduct. If there was "No prey [there was] no pay."

Injuries were compensated for, according to what was considered the most important part of a man's body. The highest sum of six hundred pieces of eight was payment for the loss of a right arm. The left arm was valued at five hundred. The right leg was worth five hundred pieces of eight but the left leg was worth only four hundred. The loss of an eye was compensated at only one hundred pieces of eight. How come? Perhaps the pirates decided you could see enough out of one eye and could afford to lose the spare.

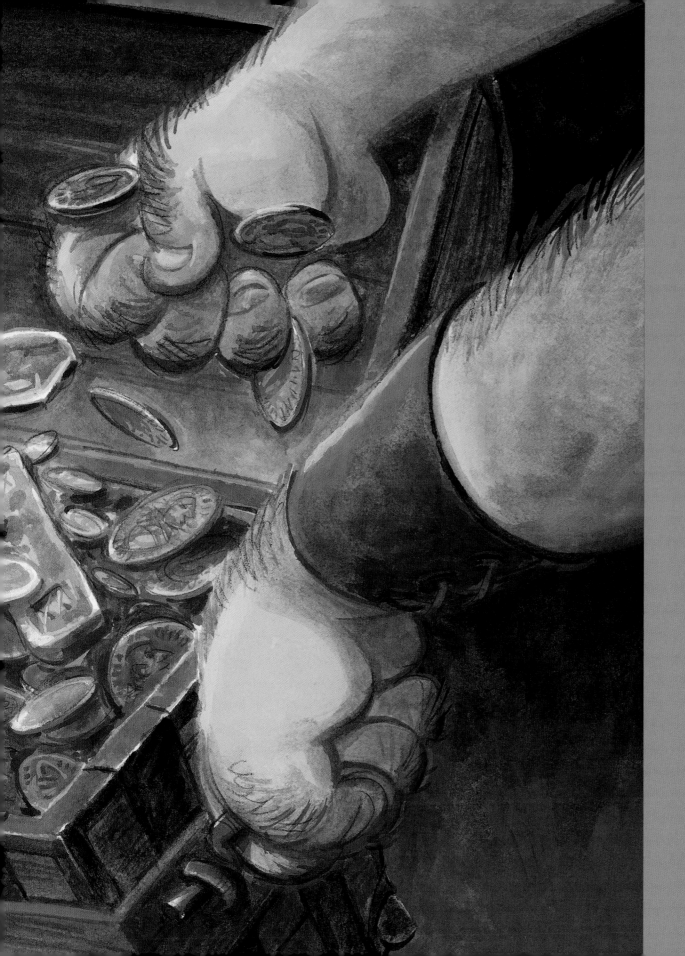

The captain got the biggest share of the booty and the rest was doled out according to the importance of each crew member. If there was a boy on board, he got a half share.

Perhaps the biggest haul ever made was taken from a captured Arab ship by the pirate Henry Avery. The prize would have been worth many millions today. Each man got a goodly share. Aargh! A likely haul for a bunch of scurvy seadogs!

Sir Henry Morgan was "lean, sallow colored, his eyes a little yellowish and belly jutting out or prominent." So said a surgeon who attended him. Certainly he wasn't handsome. But you didn't need to be good-looking to be a successful pirate. And Henry Morgan was successful.

Born in Wales he moved to Jamaica when he was a young man and "raised himself to fame and fortune by his valour." In 1665 he sailed with an expedition against Spanish settlements. When the expedition's leader was captured and executed, the crew of the ship voted Morgan to be their admiral.

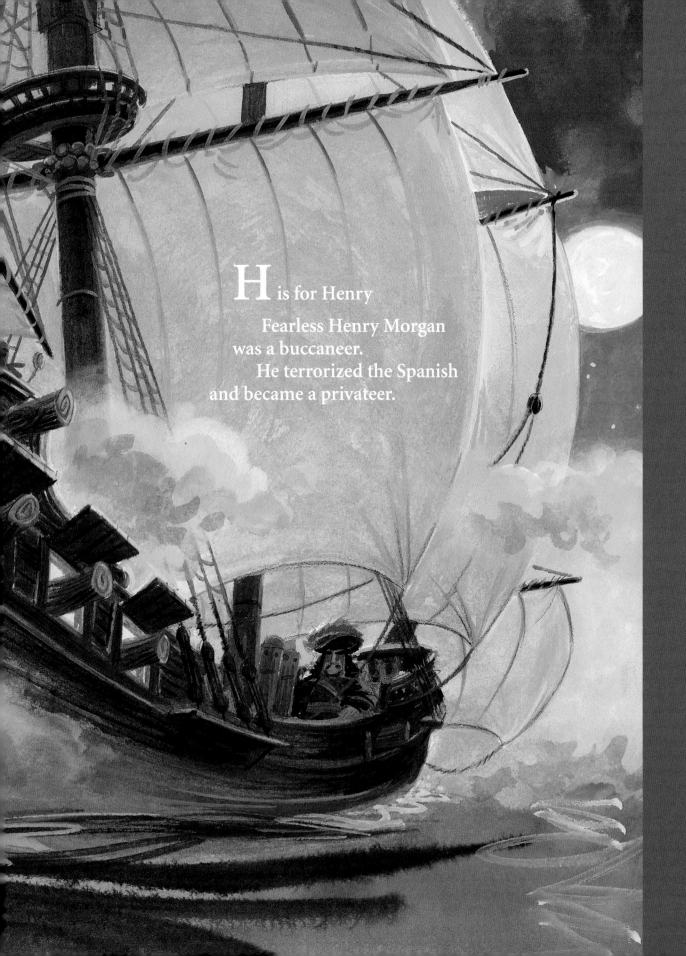

H is for Henry

Fearless Henry Morgan
was a buccaneer.
He terrorized the Spanish
and became a privateer.

Not only brave, Morgan was resourceful. On a voyage to raid the port of Maracaibo his ship was blocked by three warships of Spain's West Indian fleet. Never one to give up, Morgan disguised a Cuban merchant ship he had captured as a fearsome warship. Gunports were cut in her sides. Logs were pushed through them to look like cannons. At the rails of the ship were more logs, painted and clothed to resemble seamen. The ship was loaded with gunpowder spiked with fuses. With two small frigates behind her they headed straight for the warships. The fuses were lit and BOOM! The other two warships fled and the blockade was over.

Morgan died in 1688. He was buried in a cemetery in Jamaica. At the time of his burial the ships in the harbor at Port Royal fired their guns in tribute. After the 1692 earthquake in Jamaica, the cemetery in which he was buried was swallowed up by the sea. So, after all his exploits Henry Morgan was, in the end, "buried at sea."

What may be the remains of one of his ships has been found off the coast of Panama. The search for more knowledge of Henry Morgan, pirate, buccaneer, and privateer continues.

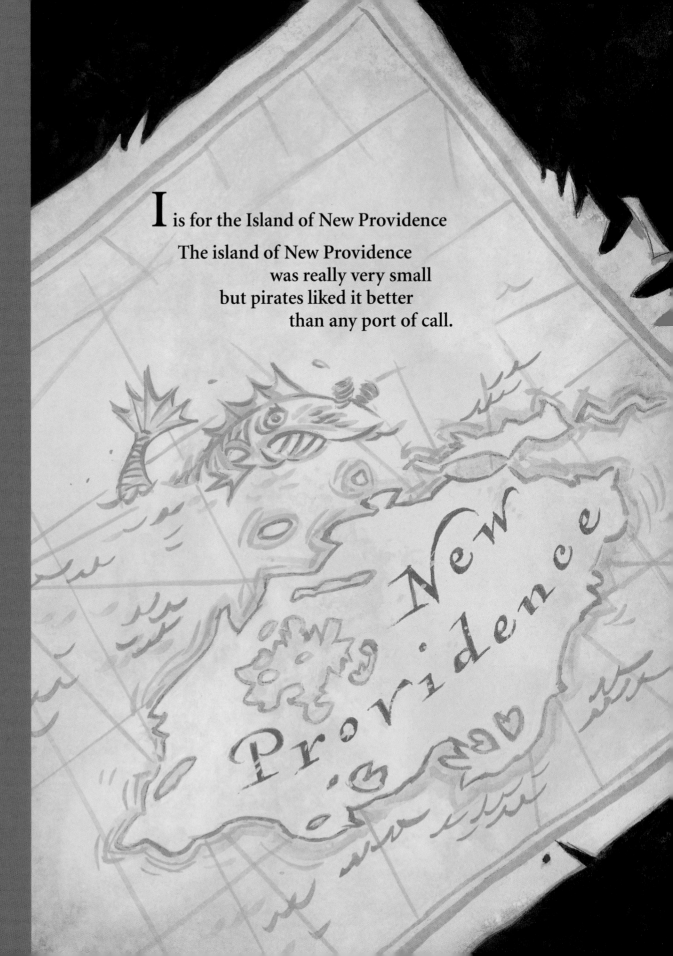

New Providence, a sixty-square-mile island in the Bahamas, was a paradise for pirates. Its harbor, surrounded by high hills, was not deep enough to allow warships to enter. But the pirate sloops with shallow draft could come and go at will. A lookout could stand on a hilltop and send warning cannon shot if an enemy was approaching, or a blast of triumph if he spotted a rich prize on the horizon. There was fresh water, fish to be caught, plenty of wildlife, and fresh fruit for the taking.

There were a few settlers on the island but they got along fine with the pirates who were generous with their ill-gotten luxuries and spent their gold freely. The capital city, Nassau, was a playground for the pirates. There they could fight with other pirates, gamble, and party with the ladies. Pirates liked ladies.

There was a saying that when a pirate slept he didn't dream that he'd died and gone to heaven. He dreamed that he'd died and returned to New Providence. Even pirates needed rest and recreation!

I i

I is for the Island of New Providence

The island of New Providence
was really very small
but pirates liked it better
than any port of call.

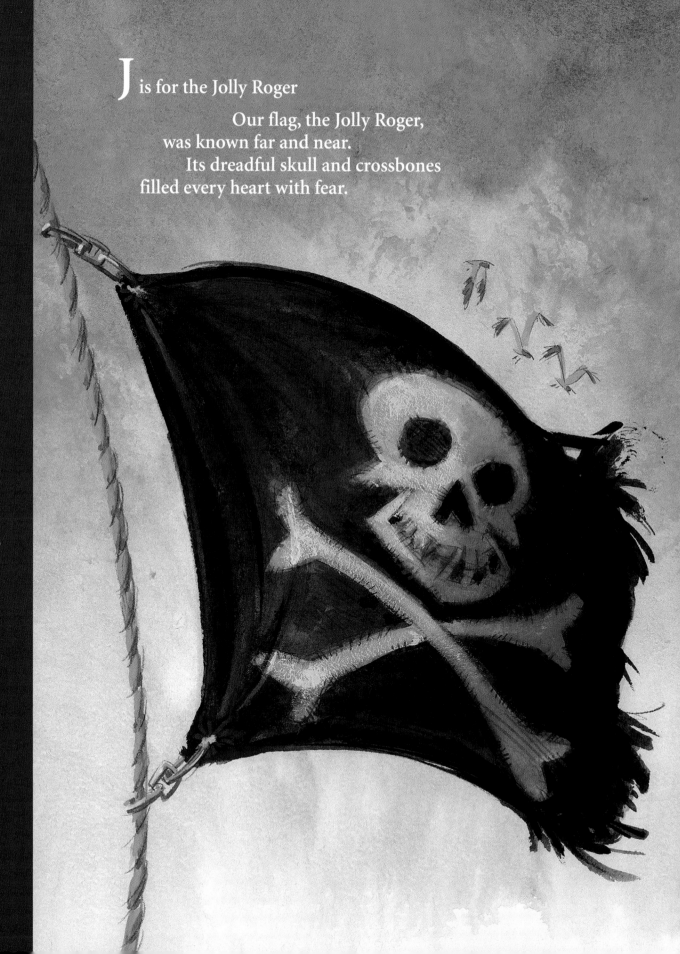

Jj

J is for the Jolly Roger

Our flag, the Jolly Roger,
was known far and near.
Its dreadful skull and crossbones
filled every heart with fear.

The Jolly Roger flag was easy to spot, flying from a mast. It showed a white skull with crossed bones on a background that was black as death.

A ship's nationality, or purpose, was known by the flag it flew. So, as it followed a ship to attack it, the pirate ship flew an innocent flag, English perhaps, or French. Only when it got within striking distance did the pirate ship hoist the Jolly Roger or its own colors.

Some pirate captains favored their own design. Blackbeard's flag showed a devil skeleton holding an hourglass in one bony hand to announce that time was running out. The other hand held an arrow that pointed at a bleeding, broken heart.

But by 1730 most pirates only flew the Jolly Roger, an all-purpose flag that was recognizable by all ships at sea. It said all that needed to be said.

Where did the name Jolly Roger come from? It may have been named after Old Roger, the devil. Jolly? Perhaps they felt that only the devil would enjoy the horrors to come.

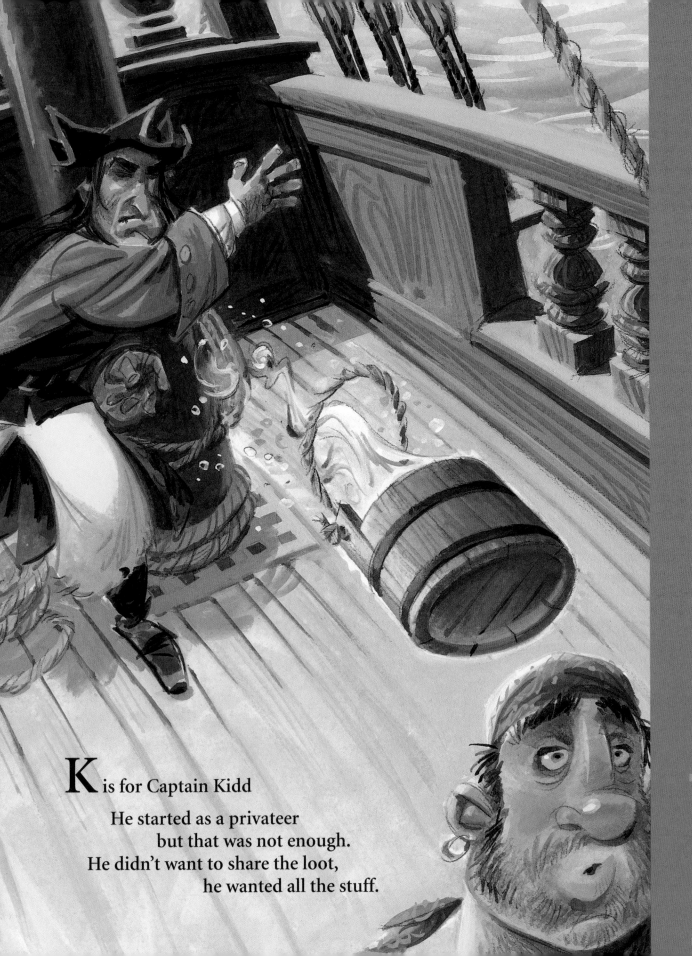

Captain William Kidd was a respectable Scotsman who in 1696 was sent by the governor of New York to capture pirate ships, steal their loot, and bring it back to New York where it could be sold.

But looking for pirates in the Indian Ocean didn't seem as profitable to Kidd as becoming a pirate himself. And *for* himself. Legend says that before he began his pirate career, he buried his family bible near Plymouth, perhaps to mark the end of his God-fearing life!

Captain Kidd spilled less blood and captured less booty than any other well-known pirate of his time. But on one of his voyages, at odds with his crew, he hit his gunner over the head with a bucket. The gunner died the next day. When Kidd was eventually captured and tried, murder was added to the piracy charges against him. He was kept in chains in Newgate Prison, said to be the most terrible of English jails. After living there for two years Kidd was tried and sentenced to death. The pirate chaser who had become a pirate was hanged in a metal harness at Execution Dock in the year 1701.

K is for Captain Kidd

He started as a privateer
but that was not enough.
He didn't want to share the loot,
he wanted all the stuff.

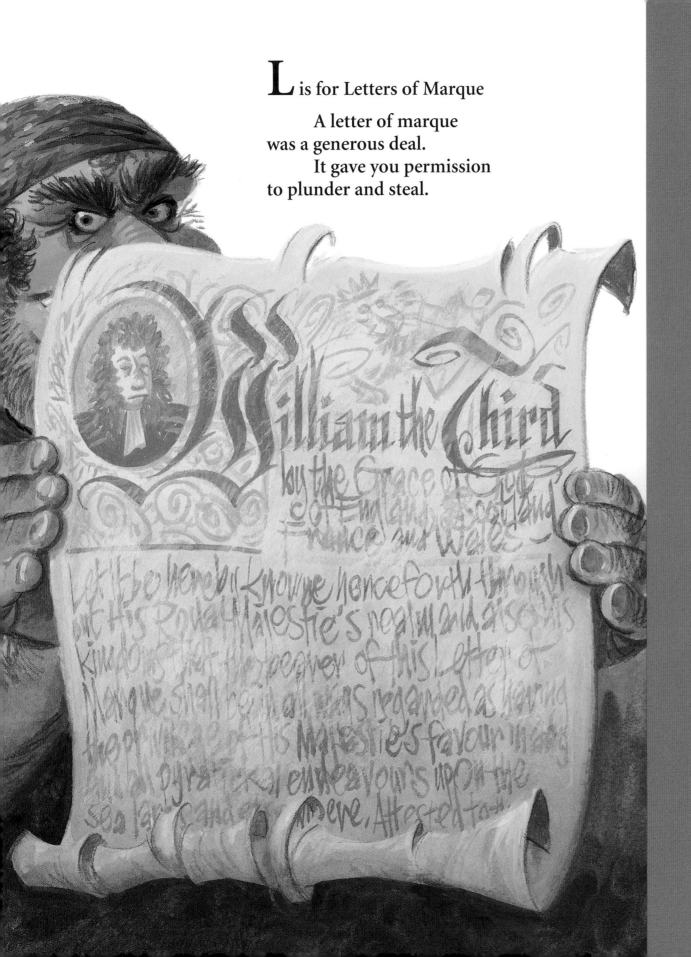

L is for Letters of Marque

A letter of marque
was a generous deal.
It gave you permission
to plunder and steal.

A letter of marque was given by the government of a country, England perhaps, or Spain or France. It permitted a privateer to attack and take enemy vessels, and bring them back to be sold or auctioned by the provider of the permission. Plunder taken was shared between the privateer and the government or sovereign.

The full term is "letter of marque and reprisal," as privateers not only seized wealth but attacked any enemies of their government at sea and shared the proceeds. Sir Francis Drake's ships attacked Spanish vessels and brought the wealth back to Queen Elizabeth I to be divided between them.

In other words, pirates (called privateers) with letters of marque could attack and steal without being charged with piracy. And if the crew was captured they were treated with respect as prisoners of war, not thieving pirates. No need to worry about Execution Dock.

In reality pirates were dirty, cruel, and, for the most part, ugly people. But not in movies. The films of the 1930s and 1940s glamorized them, made them dashing and handsome. Who was more bold and gallant than Douglas Fairbanks in *The Black Pirate*? After he captures a gigantic galleon single-handedly, the Black Pirate swings on a rope to the top of the masthead, digs his trusty knife into a sail, and rips its canvas in half as he sizzles back down to the deck. *The Black Pirate* was a silent movie, but who needed sound? In 1935 Errol Flynn starred in *Captain Blood*, a movie that had floggings, torture, and killings, all of which the audiences adored. It was a smash hit.

Many of the most famous pirate captains were the subjects of these action-packed films. *Blackbeard the Pirate* came out in 1952. *Captain Kidd* (1945) starred Charles Laughton. It was not a good movie! Few of these movies were even slightly historically accurate. But nobody cared. Audiences wanted to believe in buried treasure and "walking the plank" and handsome pirate captains. And we still do. The flashy Johnny Depp swaggers across our movie screens as cocky Captain Jack Sparrow in the *Pirates of the Caribbean* movies and we are hooked again.

M
m

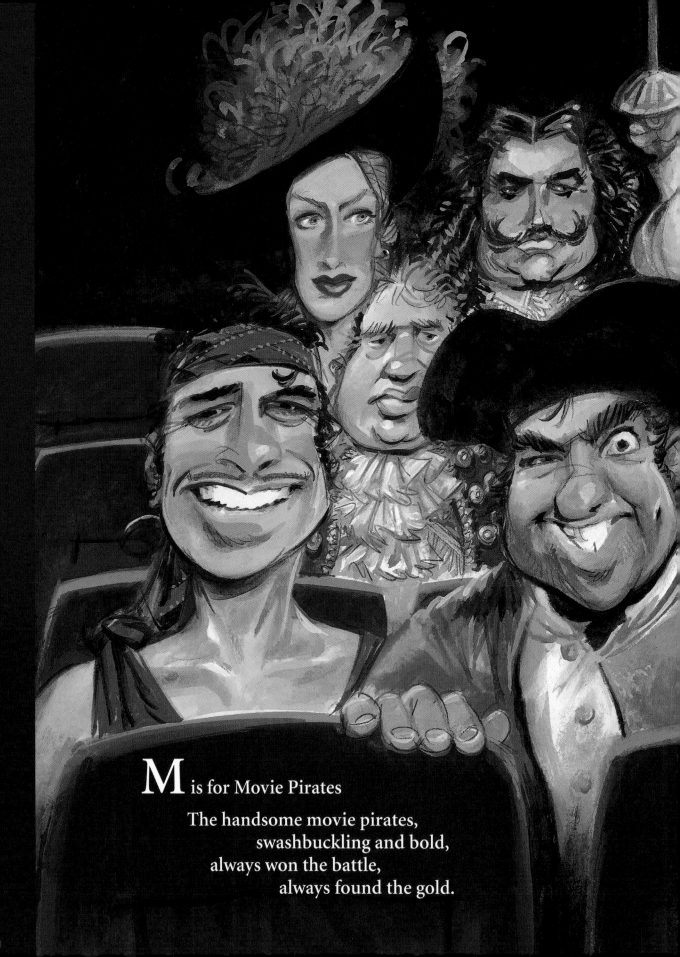

M is for Movie Pirates

The handsome movie pirates,
swashbuckling and bold,
always won the battle,
always found the gold.

N n

N is for Nassau

Nassau was a pirate base;
no other place compared.
They spent their money in the town
and got their ships repaired.

Nassau is the main port and capital of New Providence. The island had been abandoned by the British in 1704 and the pirates came and took it over. It was the greatest collection of pirates ever seen. They built houses for themselves, ate, drank, and made merry in the streets of the town. They also lived in tents, in the hulls of old abandoned ships, on street corners. It didn't matter to them. They were surrounded by pirate friends and could terrorize and take over from the legitimate residents.

The population of Nassau grew to over two thousand. Blackbeard set up his base there as did Charles Vane and Jack Rackham (Calico Jack), and countless others. They would sail in, repair their ships, spend money, and make merry. If their cash ran out they would chase and plunder another ship.

But in 1718 a naval commander, Woodes Rogers, was sent to drive out the pirates and he did. It was then made known that pirates were no longer welcome.

The captain was in charge of the ship but he wasn't as important as his name implies. He was elected by the crew and if he failed them he could be removed. On one pirate voyage the captain was changed 12 times. Only in battle did he come into his own. Then he controlled absolutely.

The quartermaster was second in command. He handled the helm when the ship was under sail and was trusted to fairly divide the plunder taken in battle. "Sails" kept the sails in good order, the blacksmith made bolts and rings for the rigging, and the carpenter repaired storm or battle damage. Since he had the same tools, saws, etc., the carpenter stood in for a surgeon when necessary. The gunner looked after the cannon, the muskets, and the pistols. The cook kept the crew fed. The musicians played for the crew, cheering them with jigs and hornpipes.

Every single pirate was a good seaman and brave and fierce in battle, his other roles forgotten.

O is for Occupations

The captain and the carpenter,
the quartermaster, too,
the navigator and the cook
were part of every crew.

The word *pirate* means "one who plunders on the sea." But there were different names for different categories of pirates.

The "privateers" were actually pirates who had been commissioned by a government to raid enemy ships and bring back the loot to be sold for a profit (See L.). They flew the flags of their countries and thought of their vessels as private warships. They were, in fact, licensed pirates.

The "buccaneers" were pirates in the seventeenth century who preyed on Spanish ships in the Caribbean. Henry Morgan was one of the most daring and ruthless of the buccaneers. When he died in Jamaica he left a wealthy estate.

Most pirates were ordinary men who had gone to sea as boys and wanted what they thought of as a life of adventure and easy riches. In the Golden Age of Piracy (early to mid-eighteenth century) unemployment was ever present. It was just a small step from poverty to the possible riches of a pirate's life.

P p

P is for Pirates

There were privateers and buccaneers—
call them any name.
All of them were pirates
in the pirate game.

Other pirates were deserters from the navies. Sometimes when pirates attacked a naval ship, they asked the sailors to leave their present ship and join theirs. Many times the offer was accepted. On other occasions pirates kidnapped lads from coastal villages to join them, willingly or unwillingly.

Pirate, privateer, buccaneer—whatever their names they were all pirates at heart.

Q

q

Q is for Queen of the Pirates, Grace O'Malley

She was the Queen of Pirates,
as brave as anyone.
She could wield a cutlass.
She could shoot a gun.

Grace O'Malley, the Queen of the Pirates, came from an Irish seafaring family. When she was a young girl, while with her father on a voyage, she saved his life by tackling an enemy pirate who was intent on murdering him. Perhaps that first taste of success in battle helped her decide on her life to come. As a pirate she attacked and plundered vessels unfortunate enough to sail along the Irish coast.

In 1577 she was captured and spent 18 months in jail in Dublin Castle. Out of jail at last, O'Malley went back to her old life of piracy and plunder. But her fleet was impounded by the order of the governor of Connaught. In 1593 O'Malley wrote to the queen of England and then went to London to personally appeal to her. There is no record of what was said between them. But the queen sent a letter to the governor ordering that O'Malley be provided with a pension for life. It is said that the two women, both strong and ruthless in a world of men, became friends.

Grace O'Malley was not the only woman pirate. There were many, including Alwinda, the daughter of a Swedish king, who became a pirate in the fifth century.

Two women, the Irish Anne Bonny and the English Mary Read, were pirates and friends in the 1700s. They served for a while on the same pirate ship. Like all female pirates they chopped off their hair, dressed, fought, and swore like men. Many of these women went unrecognized as female.

Bonny and Read were captured and tried in Port Royal, Jamaica, and were sentenced to be hanged. However, they were both expecting babies and "pleaded their bellies" and were set free. Calico Jack, the man Bonny had promised to marry, had been less than brave when their ship was captured. He was sentenced to be hanged. Going to visit him on the day of the hanging Bonny spoke her last words to him. "I'm sorry to see you there, Jack, but if you had fought like a man, you might not have been hanged like a dog." Spoken like a true pirate.

R is for Revenge (*Queen Anne's Revenge*)

It was Blackbeard's flagship
but it went aground.
After all these many years
its wreck has now been found.

The *Queen Anne's Revenge* was Blackbeard's flagship for only three years. It was a frigate, built in England but captured one year later by the French, and renamed *La Concorde*. Captured again, this time by pirates under the command of Captain Benjamin Hornigold, the ship was given to one of his favored men and the man was made captain. The new captain was Edward Teach, known as Blackbeard. Renamed again as *Queen Anne's Revenge* it became Blackbeard's flagship.

In the spring of 1718 Blackbeard blockaded Charleston (called Charles Town at the time) and seized eight ships sailing in and out of the harbor. He kept the best of them. By June of that same year he had a fleet of four ships and about four hundred men but soon afterward the *Queen Anne's Revenge* went aground off North Carolina's coast. It was said that Blackbeard, a skillful sailor, gave orders to the helmsman to take a course that steered the ship into the shoals. It is unclear why, though many think he wanted to get rid of his crew.

In November 1996 a private research firm discovered the wreck of the *Queen Anne's Revenge* off North Carolina. More than 1,600 artifacts from the ship have been discovered. In 2011 the massive ship's anchor was brought to the surface.

R r

Pirate ships had to be fast. In your wicked life you were either chasing one ship or fleeing from another. It was also advantageous to have a ship with a shallow draft (a draft was the bulk of the hull and keel that was underwater). A shallow draft allowed the ship to sail into coves with shallow water where it could not be followed.

Many of the pirate vessels were merchant ships that the pirate crew had captured and adapted to their own needs. It was good to "trade up" and hijack a better ship for yourself if you came across one! A pirate captain might hijack several ships and be in command of three or four vessels of differing shapes and sizes.

A schooner was a narrow vessel with two masts, fore and aft (front and back). She was speedy with a shallow draft. Some were big enough to have a crew of 75.

A frigate was square-rigged on all three

Merchant Ship

S is for Ships

Schooners, sloops
both big and small.
Greedy pirates
loved them all.

Sloop

Schooner

Brigantine

Frigate

A frigate was square-rigged on all three masts. She was fast and carried her guns on her upper decks.

A brigantine was slow but big. She was good for long voyages and for intimidating smaller ships. With lots of cargo space she could carry a great deal of plundered booty.

The sloop was the pirates' favorite ship. It had all the requirements they needed. It had a bowsprit (a thick pole sticking out from the bow) almost as long as its body. In addition, a square topsail gave it great speed. Its draft was not as shallow as that of a schooner but its speed and nimble movements made it very desirable.

It is interesting that most ships are referred to as "she." And they have been since ships first went to sea. Perhaps the reason is that ships are so often given women's names. In 1497, for instance, Christopher Columbus named one of his ships the *Filipa*, perhaps after his wife, Filipa. Or it may be that men on ships, parted from wives and mothers, like the comfort of a female to keep them safe.

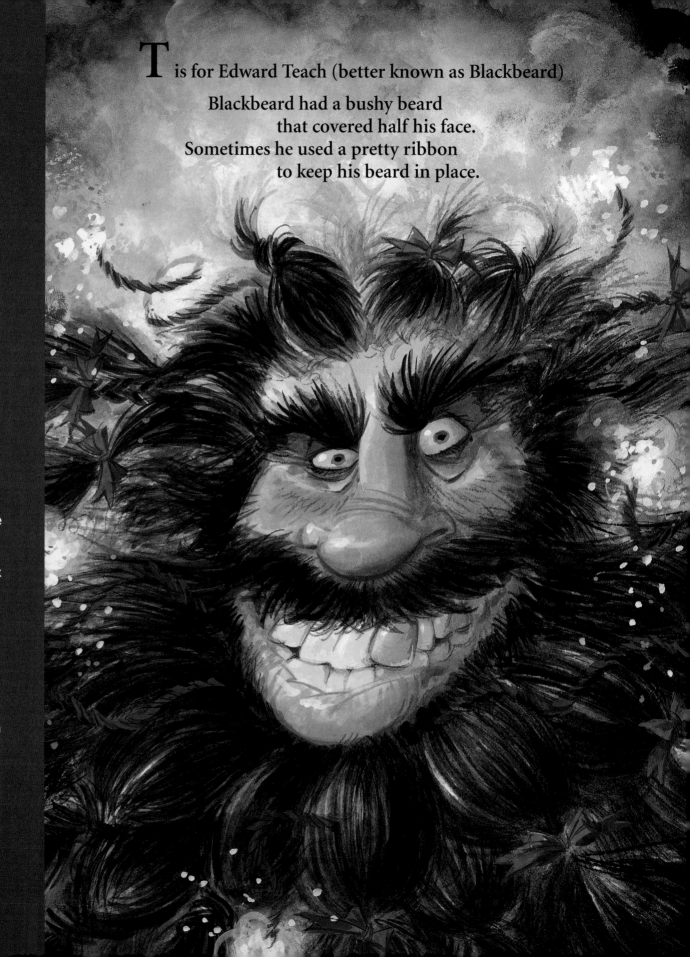

T t

T is for Edward Teach (better known as Blackbeard)

Blackbeard had a bushy beard
that covered half his face.
Sometimes he used a pretty ribbon
to keep his beard in place.

Blackbeard was one of the most feared of pirates. His appearance alone could strike terror into the hearts of anyone unfortunate enough to be his captive.

His real name was Edward Teach. His pirate name came from his bush of a black beard that was long to his chest, came over his face to his eyes, and spread out like a black angel's halo on either side. He liked to tie small red bows in it. Or make curly pigtails to tuck behind his ears. To look even more terrifying he'd stick pieces of hemp under his hat and set them on fire so that his entire head would seem to be ablaze.

One night, playing cards on his ship with a friend, he pulled out his pistol and shot him in the knee. Why? "If I do not now and then kill one of you you'll forget who I am," he answered. So much for friendship.

The day he was captured, while boarding a navy ship, Blackbeard kept firing his three pistols even though he had been saber-slashed 20 times. Badly wounded, he was eventually killed.

A pirate ship had to be fast and nimble to evade enemies or capture prizes. Seaweed and barnacles and other little sea creatures stuck underneath the hull slowed it down. Since a pirate ship could not be hauled up out of the water and into an honest dock to have its hull scraped, the crew had to "careen" it every few months.

The vessel was dragged on to some solitary beach at low tide. Using a block and tackle it was pulled onto its side (careened) and the exposed bottom scraped to get rid of whatever was stuck fast underneath. The bottom was then painted with mixtures of tallow and brimstone to discourage more unwanted sea creatures. Planks that had been damaged in battles or storms were replaced. The rats that had been hiding in the bilges (the lowest inside part of the hull) were chased out, and the ship would be hauled back into the ocean, ready to sail again, free of its unwanted passengers.

U u

U is for Underneath

Underneath a pirate ship
where nobody could see
were sticky little creatures,
clinging secretly.

V is for Charles Vane

He was captured, but escaped
            to plunder and to kill.
But after that, his pirate luck
            went suddenly downhill.

Charles Vane was an English pirate, well known for his cruelty. In a sea filled with brutal pirates, he was the worst. He tortured or killed captives and ignored the pirate code he had sworn to. He abused and stole from his own crew. On his flagship, *Ranger*, he was despised.

But a captain can be voted out by his crew and Vane was driven out by his. He was happily set adrift in a small ship but he lived on, came back and continued pirating. His ship was wrecked in a storm and Vane, one of the only survivors, was washed up on an uninhabited island. He thought he was to be saved when another ship came, commanded by Captain Holford. Unfortunately for Vane, Captain Holford knew him and wouldn't pick him up.

Another ship did, but again it was bad luck or justice or both that the second ship's captain and Captain Holford were friends. Holford recognized Vane, took him back on board his own ship, locked him in the brig, and then turned him over to the authorities.

Vane was hanged at Gallows Point in Port Royal in 1721. "A short drop and a quick stop," as the pirates called it. Not many mourned his death.

The *Whydah* was an armed English merchant ship. She was one of the largest of naval vessels, heavily armed with eighteen six-pounder guns. Her captain was Lawrence Prince. Leaving Port Royal to sail back to England loaded with a valuable cargo, his ship was attacked and taken over by the pirate vessel, *Marianne*, under its captain Sam Bellamy. "Black Sam" used the *Whydah* well, stealing and plundering other ships. Its name and his were well known in pirate waters. But off the treacherous coast of Cape Cod on a voyage to Provincetown, the *Whydah* was the victim of a deadly storm. The *Whydah* ran aground, killing 160 men, including Bellamy.

The wreck of the *Whydah* was found in 1984 by underwater explorer Barry Clifford. His team has recovered numerous artifacts from the wreck, including the ship's bell with the inscription THE WHYDAH GALLEY 1716 engraved on it. Weapons, musket balls, grenades, and personal belongings have been found.

W
W

W is for the *Whydah*

The *Whydah* was a pirate ship
that sank beneath the sea.
Its broken hull has now been found,
a part of history.

"X marks the spot" is a common saying and is supposed to relate to the way pirates marked a map with an X to show where treasure was buried. Except that only one pirate is known to have buried his loot ... Captain Kidd. But the legend persists.

Pirates seldom accumulated treasure. They spent gold as fast as they got it. Their motto was "live for today; there may be no tomorrow."

Their lives were so dangerous and the possibility of hanging so close that they didn't hoard their treasure, they enjoyed it. On shore they spent freely, sold whatever booty they had plundered, and had themselves a rip-roaring good time.

If treasure had ever been buried it is certain no map was left. And no spot would have been X'd. More money has been spent searching for buried treasure than ever was found.

X

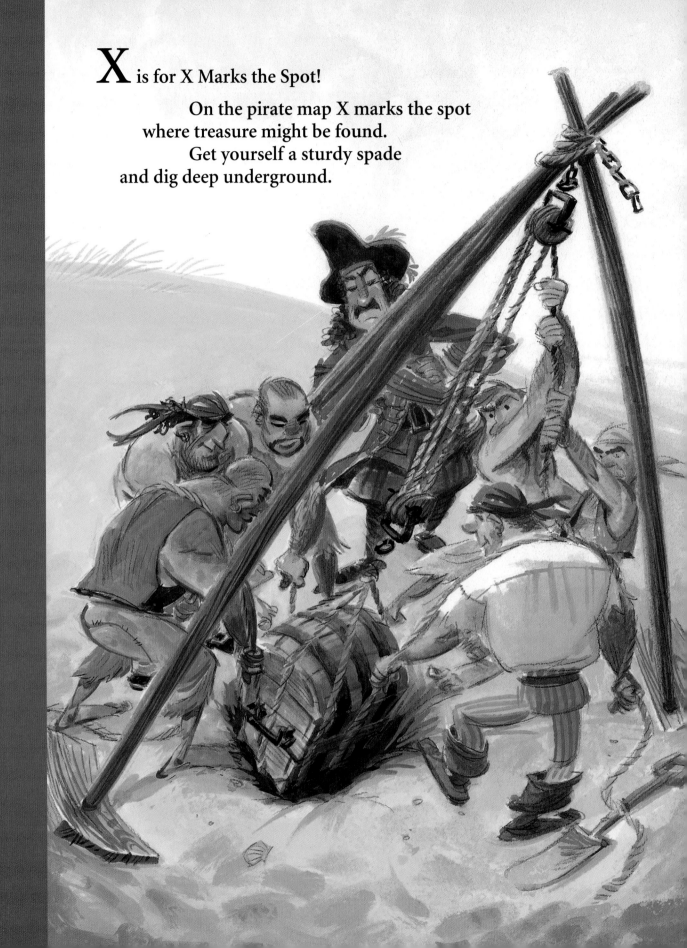

X is for X Marks the Spot!

On the pirate map X marks the spot
where treasure might be found.
Get yourself a sturdy spade
and dig deep underground.

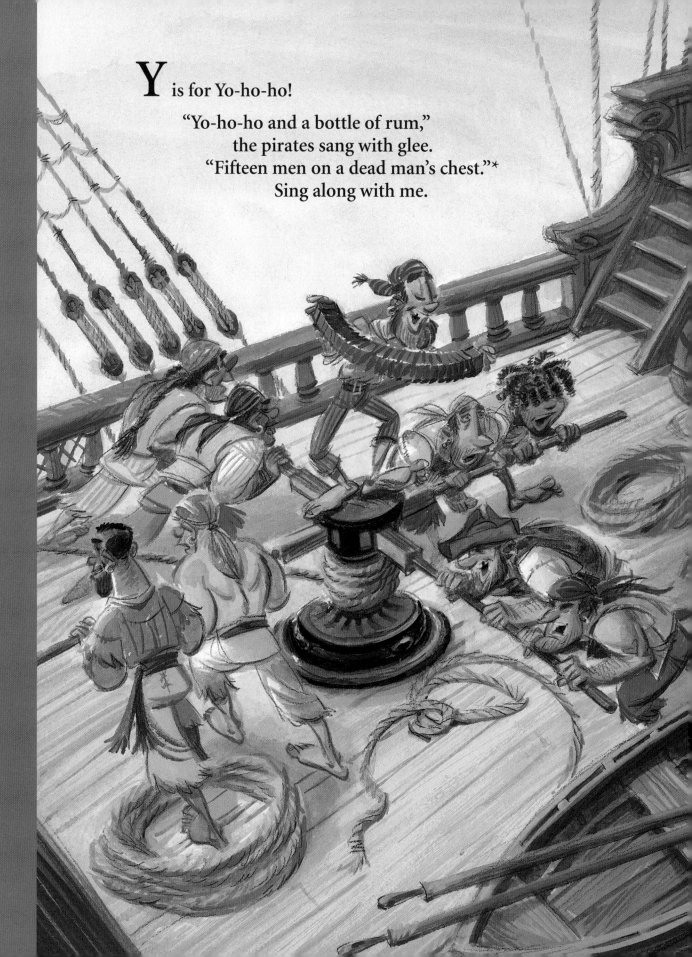

Yy

Y is for Yo-ho-ho!

"Yo-ho-ho and a bottle of rum,"
the pirates sang with glee.
"Fifteen men on a dead man's chest."*
Sing along with me.

"Yo-ho-ho, it's a pirate's life for me!" What a great, rousing song!

"Fifteen men on a dead man's chest." His treasure chest? Or his chest that they sat on to make sure he wasn't still breathing? No matter. It was a great "pull-together" song.

Sea shanties rollicked along, singing of happy-go-lucky lives, riches, and the ladies.

"What shall we do with the drunken sailor?" or "Way, hey, blow the man down."

Or perhaps "Up aloft the yard must go. Up aloft from down below."

Shanties were sung by pirates as they did their backbreaking work aboard ship in nasty weather and stormy seas. The songs helped keep up their spirits. The rhythm made the work go better. "Get to singing," a quartermaster might shout if the labor went too slowly. They did.

In *Redburn: His First Voyage*, Herman Melville wrote, "I soon got used to the singing; for the sailors never touched a rope without it."

* From Robert Louis Stevenson's "Dead Man's Chest," which appeared in *Treasure Island*.

"Zounds!" was an expression of awe and wonderment, comparable to "Wow!" "Shiver me timbers!" was almost the same, a pirate showing surprise. No flabbergasted pirate would ever say, "Golly gee!" And then there was "Aargh!," an all-purpose word that shouted, "You've insulted me, ye bilge rat!" Or "Ye're all right, matey!" Every meaning depended on the tone of voice or the scowl, or scorn or bellow of laughter that went with it. *Aargh!*

There were plenty of pirate insults: "Ye're a swabbie!" Or "Ye scurvy dog!" Or even "Ye bilge rat!" There were enticing invitations to the ladies when they met up with them on shore. "C'mere, me beauty!" Or invitations to other pirates to keep on drinking. "Drink up, me hearties!" It was a short life and a merry one.

"Give no quarter" meant show no mercy and was frequently used.

Z z

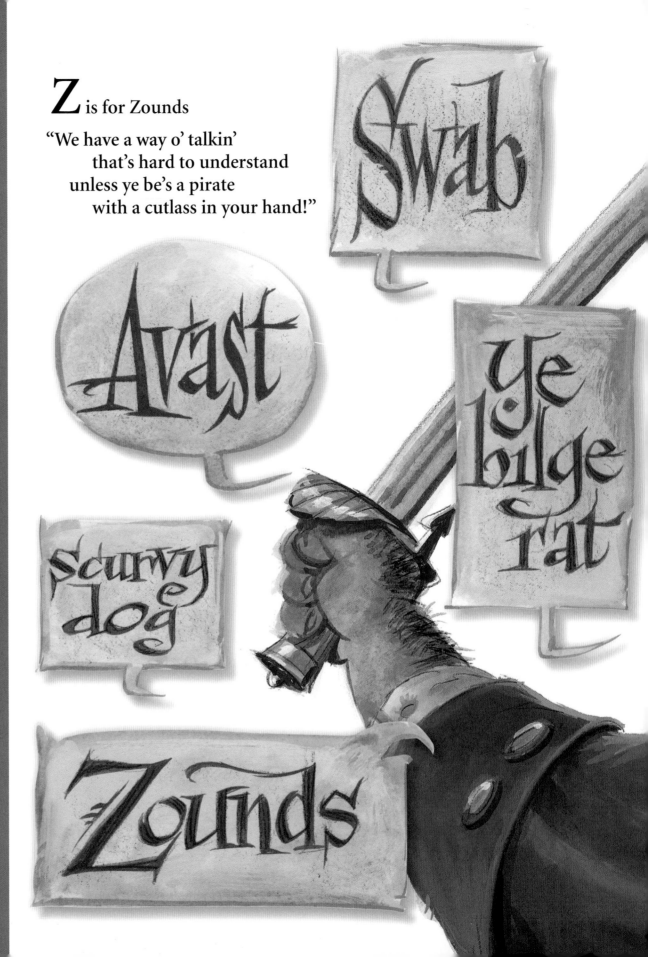

Z is for Zounds

"We have a way o' talkin'
    that's hard to understand
unless ye be's a pirate
    with a cutlass in your hand!"

"Blow the man down!" was just another way of saying, "Kill the scurvy dog!" and when the deed was done, they could announce with satisfaction, "Dead men tell no tales" and perhaps join in singing along with "Fifteen men on a dead man's chest." Very jovial!

If you still want to be a pirate, you can learn the lingo during "Talk Like a Pirate Day" on September 19 every year.

Well, shiver me timbers and furl the sails, we've come to the end of the alphabet. "Batten down the hatches!" It's been a long, long voyage, but there's land ahead. "So fair winds to ye, me hearty, when ye sail again."

Ahoy, Ye Landlubbers!

How Many Questions Can Ye Answer?

What is the name of the short, broad, slashing sword used by pirates?

Where was Davy Jones's Locker?

Who was the "Queen of the Pirates"?

Which terrible pirate had a great black beard and tied red bows in it?

What did the word "careening" mean?

Which pirate crewman worked as surgeon when necessary?

Was the "Jolly Roger" a pirate flag or a happy pirate called Roger?

What happened to the *Whydah*, an armed English merchant ship?

What was meant by the code of conduct? Name one rule.

Which pirate captain is said to have buried his treasure (booty)?

Finally, can you guess the names of the movie pirates sitting in the theater (See M)?
The answer to this question is below.

First row: Johnny Depp as Captain Jack Sparrow in *Pirates of the Caribbean* (2006). Second row: Douglas Fairbanks in *The Black Pirate* (1926); Robert Newton as Long John Silver in *Treasure Island* (1950); Errol Flynn as Peter Blood in *Captain Blood* (1935). Third row: Charles Laughton as Captain Kidd in *Captain Kidd* (1945); Charlton Heston as Long John Silver in *Treasure Island* (1990); Dustin Hoffman as Captain Hook in *Hook* (1991); Walter Matthau as Captain Red in *Pirates* (1986). Fourth row: Maureen O'Hara as Prudence 'Spitfire' Stevens in *Against All Flags* (1952); Laird Cregar as Sir Henry Morgan in *The Black Swan* (1942); Kevin Kline as the Pirate King in *The Pirates of Penzance* (1983); Graham Chapman as Captain Yellowbeard in *Yellowbeard* (1983).